TILLY'S PONY TAILS

Red Admiral
the racehorse

TILLY'S PONY TAILS

Red Admiral
the racehorse

PIPPA FUNNELL

Illustrated by Jennifer Miles

Orion
Children's Books

First published in Great Britain in 2009
by Orion Children's Books
a division of the Orion Publishing Group Ltd
Orion House
5 Upper St Martin's Lane
London WC2H 9EA
An Hachette UK Company

3 5 7 9 8 6 4

A catalogue record for this book is available from the British Library.

ISBN 978 1 84255 710 5

Printed and bound in the UK by CPI Mackays, Chatham ME5 8TD

www.orionbooks.co.uk

For my mother,
Jenny Nolan

One

Tilly Redbrow was mad about horses. Her favourite way to spend time was at Silver Shoe Farm. In fact, it was like a second home to her. Ever since Tilly helped rescue a mysterious horse called Magic Spirit, she had been a regular visitor.

As often as she could, Tilly would be there, helping Angela, who ran the stables. Over the months, Tilly learned how to groom and muck out. She'd made new friends called Cally and Mia, and helped them to care for Rosie – the pretty strawberry roan pony they shared. But what Tilly liked most of all, was spending time with Magic Spirit. She had a special friendship with him. Tilly was the person Magic Spirit trusted most, and although he'd been underweight and unhappy when he'd arrived at the stables, he was growing stronger and healthier by the week. One day he was going to be a fabulous horse.

Tilly loved helping to care for the horses, but what she was really looking forward to was learning how to ride. Every time she saw people getting ready in the yard, saddling up and heading out on some of the forest hacks, or going to the indoor school for lessons, she longed to be doing the same.

 The chance of a ride was all she could think about as she sat down for breakfast, twiddling the horsehair bracelet she'd worn all her life. It was Saturday, so the whole family were at the table, chatting and taking their time.

"Good morning, dreamy," said Tilly's mum, passing her the cereal. Tilly always chose muesli with chopped banana, followed by a big glass of orange juice.

Mr Redbrow looked up from his newspaper and smiled.

"Morning, Tiger Lil'. The weather's going to be lovely today. What about a fishing trip to the river with me and Adam?" he asked, with a wink.

Adam was Tilly's younger brother. He was busy flicking bits of toast across the table. He was annoying in the way that little brothers sometimes can be.

All Tilly wanted to do was spend the day with the horses. It was the first hot day in May, and she knew the stable yard was going to be buzzing with activity. Adam just grinned at her and poked out his tongue.

"But I guess you'll be going to Silver Shoe Farm," her dad continued, as if he was reading her mind. "Adam and I will have to go fishing on our own. You know, some parents complain that their children sit around doing nothing at the weekend! Not you though, eh, Tilly? You're always doing something – as long as it involves horses!"

Tilly caught her dad's eye. Despite what he said, she knew that really he was happy for her, and proud of her hard work. He understood what horses meant to her.

"Oh, look," said Tilly's mum, studying the date at the top of the newspaper. "It's nearly the end of the month. Not long till your birthday, Tilly. Perhaps you'll want a sleepover? Have you thought about what you want for a present yet?"

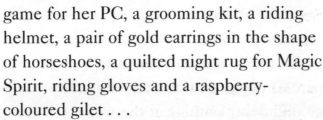

Tilly had a huge list in her mind: another year's subscription to *Pony* magazine, a pair of canary yellow jodhpurs, a copy of *Pony Ranch!* game for her PC, a grooming kit, a riding helmet, a pair of gold earrings in the shape of horseshoes, a quilted night rug for Magic Spirit, riding gloves and a raspberry-coloured gilet . . .

She shut her eyes and reeled off the list. Then she decided to go for the big one.

"Riding lessons – at the farm. It would be extra great if you could get me those!"

"Hmm, we'll have to see about that," said her mum, exchanging glances with Mr Redbrow.

Underneath the table, Tilly had her fingers crossed.

Just then, her phone buzzed. She pulled it out of her pocket and checked the message. She knew straightaway that it would be from either Mia or Cally.

PERFECT DAY. IF U R NOT AT THE FARM BY 10AM
THEN U R A LOSER! LOVE MIA XXX

Tilly laughed.

"Dad," she said, as she swallowed a mouthful of muesli. "If you're taking Adam fishing soon, then can you give me a lift to Silver Shoe Farm on your way?"

"Whatever you say, Tiger Lil'."

"Thanks, Dad!"

12

Two

They drove along the now familiar
leafy lane that led to Silver Shoe Farm.
Eventually they pulled up at the five-bar
gate and Tilly said goodbye to her dad and
Adam. She marched across the yard,
straight to Magic Spirit's large stable, which
was more like a barn, situated at the back
of the yard. Sure enough, there he was,
happily munching some hay.

"Hello, boy!" she said. She couldn't
believe how well he was looking. He had

put on weight, his coat was getting its shine back and most of the sores had gone. Tilly remembered going into his stable for the first time. Back then his coat had been matted and filthy. His eyes had been wild and his whole body tense. He had startled and nearly knocked her over. Today, he was peaceful and relaxed. It was almost as though he was a different horse.

Magic Spirit looked up at Tilly and immediately came towards her. His ears pricked forward at the sound of her voice.

"You do look handsome," she said, stroking his neck proudly. Magic Spirit nuzzled her shoulder.

Duncan, Angela's head boy, appeared in the doorway with some mucking out tools.

"Hello, guys. I thought I'd find you in here, Tilly. I saw your dad drop you off. Just in time . . ."

Tilly saw that he was holding a shovel and bucket.

"Do you think you'd be able to muck out Magic Spirit's stable and then give him a brush down?"

"Sure," said Tilly eagerly.

"You can tie him up outside."

"Where's his head collar?" asked Tilly, noticing that Magic Spirit wasn't wearing one.

"I've got a smart new leather one," said Duncan, handing it to Tilly. "Do you want to see if it fits?"

Tilly approached Magic, chatting away and telling him what she was about to do, as if he understood her every word. She knew he didn't like sudden movements around his head, so she reassured him by rubbing his favourite spot at the base of his wither.

Before putting the head collar on him, she undid the clip attached to the strap under the throat, and let the headpiece out onto the last hole so it would be easier to get on. Then she slipped the noseband over Magic's nose and quietly pulled the headpiece over his ears. Once it was in place, she clipped the throat strap back and adjusted the buckle, so it was two holes tighter, but not too tight. She had seen from pictures that head collars were fitted more loosely than bridles.

Magic Spirit stood very still, and even helped a little by lowering his head.

"That's it," said Duncan, watching her. "Gently swing the head strap behind Magic's ears, but be careful not to drag it over his eyes, ears, or nose."

Duncan clipped the lead rope to the ring on the underside of the halter and offered it to Tilly. Her stomach filled with butterflies. She reached for the rope, but she was so excited and overwhelmed by the thought of actually leading Magic Spirit

by herself, she could hardly move. She just
stared at him adoringly.

"Go for it," urged Duncan.

He showed her how to hold the rope,
avoiding looping it around her own hand.

"If the rope is looped around your hand
you risk getting rope burns if he pulls
away," he explained. "Now, stand at his
shoulder and give him his cue. I usually
give one click and then say 'walk on' which
he seems to respond to. Although he
doesn't seem to have been broken in yet,
he's obviously had some experience of
being led in the past."

"How old do you think he is?" asked
Tilly.

"He's a four year old – still young."
Duncan had looked at Magic's teeth once
he'd become calm enough to handle.
"That's how you judge a horse's age," he
explained.

Tilly positioned herself at Magic Spirit's
shoulder, and smiled at him. He gave her a
little nod, as if to say, 'I'm ready'. In her

head she counted to three then clicked once and spoke out loud:

"Walk on, boy."

It was clear that Magic Spirit understood. He walked forward without any further prompting.

"That's perfect," said Duncan, behind them. "You've got such a good way with horses, Tilly."

As they walked together into the sunlight, Tilly beamed with pride. The smell of honeysuckle and freshly-mown grass drifted towards them.

Even though it was only a short distance to the tie-up ring on the far wall, Tilly's confidence grew with every step and it felt as though they'd covered a large amount of ground.

"Whoa, boy!"

Together Magic Spirit and Tilly stood still, and Duncan caught up with them.

"Great. Now, allow a length of rope so that he's free to move and look around, not too long . . . and then I'll show you how to tie him safely."

Duncan took the rope from Tilly and demonstrated a quick release knot. Tilly watched closely, but she was still a bit confused.

"Don't worry," laughed Duncan, seeing the expression on her face. "It takes practice. If you join the Pony Club and get some riding lessons you'll learn all the skills you need. But if you're not sure about something, you can always ask. It's better to ask than take a risk."

Tilly wondered what the chance of getting lessons would be. Maybe for her birthday? She hoped her mum and dad would agree that it was a good idea – she'd do anything. Everybody's chores for a week, a hundred hours of homework . . . she'd even sell some of her old My Little Pony toy collection (which she had started when she was five) – it didn't seem quite so cool, now that she had the real thing standing next to her!

Three

After mucking out the stable and grooming
Magic Spirit, Tilly met up with her friends,
Cally and Mia. They'd finished grooming
Rosie and were in the club room, making
lemonade.

"Real lemons and loads of sugar," said
Mia, as she poured the ingredients into a
jug.

"It's the yummiest thing," added Cally.
"We always make it whenever there's a
sunny weekend. It gives us energy.

We're going to have a canter this afternoon
– there's a really nice wide route around the
edge of the fields and it's dried up enough
now after the wet spring. I'm taking Rosie,
and Mia's riding a dapple grey Connemara
called Bunny."

"Bunny belongs to Zoe Lampeter,"
explained Mia. "She's another girl at the
stables, but she's staying with her mum in
America so she hasn't been able to ride for
weeks. Zoe's mum asked if we'd exercise
Bunny until she gets back."

"You're so lucky," said Tilly. "I wish
I could go riding with you this afternoon."

"Why don't you ask Angela if you can?" said Cally excitedly. "She might let you come if one of us leads you."

"Let's down our lemonade and then go and ask her!"

Angela was just about to go into the sand school with one of her horses. Cally asked whether there was a chance that Tilly might go out with her and Mia, but Angela shook her head.

"I'm sorry, Tilly, but all the ponies and horses are out – the ones that would be safe for you to ride anyway. And I think you should have some lessons in the school first. It's just not possible today."

Tilly couldn't hide her disappointment. She stared at the ground and played with one of her plaits. Cally and Mia looked disappointed too.

"I tell you what," said Angela encouragingly. "If you can get here tomorrow afternoon, about two o'clock, we could sort something out for then. I've had a cancellation of a private lesson, so I could spend the time with you and go over the basics. Call it my way of thanking you for all your hard work with Magic Spirit. Would that be okay?"

Tilly's disappointment turned into happiness. She could barely speak to say thank you. She nodded her head and grinned. Cally and Mia gave her a hug, and together the three of them jumped up and down with excitement.

"Wow! A private lesson with Angela," whispered Mia. "And you said you thought we were lucky! She knows everything there is to know about riding!"

"I'd better get started," called Angela. "And you girls should go and get tacked up if you want to make the most of the good weather. What about you, Tilly? As you're not riding, maybe you could go and see how my dad's getting on with Red Admiral. He came from Ben Hedges' yard – he's a well-known trainer of National Hunt horses, you know, horses who jump steeplechase fences and hurdles. You'll find them in the wash box, where Dad is endlessly hosing Red Admiral's leg. He got a tendon injury at his very first race meeting. He stumbled as he landed after one of the hurdles and one of his hind legs struck into his front causing a very serious injury. The vet reckons it's unlikely he'll ever race again. The owners sent him to us

eight months ago, as a last resort, to see if
we can get him right . . . maybe he needs
some of your special magic, Tilly."

Cally and Mia disappeared into the tack
room, and Tilly headed for the washbox in
the main yard. She could find her way
round the stables easily now, because every
night she lay awake thinking about it.
Every little corner of the yard was clear in
her mind.

She could see Jack Fisher with Red
Admiral. Red was the most magnificent
looking thoroughbred, a very red chestnut
with a copper gleam to his coat and a white
blaze on his nose.

Even standing in the washbox, Tilly
thought he had a regal manner, a look that
said 'I'm going to be king of the race course'.

Jack was busy hosing Red's injured leg,
and talking to the vet. It was clear from

the leg's size, below the knee down to the fetlock, that it was more filled than the other one. Jack sighed. He'd spent five months walking Red in hand, hosing his leg twice a day. Over the last three months, his work had been stepped up, putting Duncan in the saddle. Yesterday Red had had his

first piece of fast work, but today it didn't look good. His leg had filled again and looked swollen, and he was walking shorter, not wanting to put weight on it.

Four

The vet was a tall man called Brian. He
and Jack Fisher were obviously old friends.
They chatted and joked about all sorts of
things, mainly to do with horse racing.
Tilly climbed onto a bale of hay and sat
down. The men didn't notice her, as she
watched and listened to their conversation.

She learned that Jack was working with
four young thoroughbreds at the stables,
including Red Admiral. Each of them was
actually owned by someone different. He

was responsible for rehabilitating and looking after them. Tilly couldn't believe it when she heard how much money the horses were worth. Red Admiral, in particular, had been valued at £100,000 before his accident. That was more money than she could possibly imagine. She nearly gasped out loud.

"He's one of the best we've had," said Jack. "Great breeding – his sire was a former champion. The Brigdales have high hopes for him."

Tilly assumed the Brigdales must be Red Admiral's owners.

"He's cost them a small fortune. They're

shattered about the news he may not race again, so I'll do everything I can to get him back. If he comes back, he's sure to make them some big money . . ."

Brian raised his eyebrows.

"Impressive," he said.

"Absolutely," agreed Jack, scratching his belly. "Trouble is, that tendon is still not a hundred percent. End of June, we wanted to run him at the Cosford race meeting."

"Well, as I said," explained the vet. "I've got no concerns. I've checked him over and the ultrasound scan suggests the tendon will be fine. I think the swelling is from stretching the scar tissue, having galloped for all that time. Keep hosing and icing it. I guess it's up to him now."

"If he doesn't get it together, The Brigdales are going to be disappointed. All that money they've invested . . ."

"It's not just money that's at stake though, is it, Jack?" said Brian. "It's all your time and hard work."

Jack let out a long breath.

"The Brigdales told me if I can get Red Admiral sound and fit, I can keep him and train him here. They won't send him back to Ben Hedges' place. But if I can't get him fit enough to race, he'll be retired and given to Cavendish Hall as a school horse. He has such a wonderful temperament, but it would be a tragic waste."

Tilly realised that perhaps she wasn't meant to hear this part of the conversation. She slipped down from the hay bale and sneaked into the yard. It was quiet outside, because everyone had gone hacking. A broom was resting against the wall, so she picked it up and began sweeping.

As she swept, she thought about what she had overheard. She felt bad for Jack –

she knew Silver Shoe deserved to have a special horse like Red Admiral, and she knew that Jack had always dreamed of training a winner. He wouldn't take a risk with a horse that wasn't ready. Then she remembered what Angela had said to her: 'some of your special magic might help'. What did she mean by that? Tilly leaned against the broom handle and twiddled with her horsehair bracelet. Perhaps she needed to spend some quiet time with Red Admiral.

Eventually, Jack and the vet went over to the club room. When they had gone, Tilly went back into the stables. She unbolted the door and crept inside. It took a while for her eyes to adjust to the sudden darkness, and for a moment, she couldn't see anything. She found Red Admiral in his stable looking sorry for himself.

"Oh, Red Admiral. You poor thing," she whispered gently. "I hear you've hurt your leg. Let me have a look."

At first, Red Admiral didn't respond, but when she held out her arm, she noticed his ears prick up. He walked towards her and as soon as he was close enough, started sniffing at her horsehair bracelet.

"How strange!" exclaimed Tilly. "That's exactly what Magic Spirit likes to do."

He worked his nose around the bracelet and then along her arm, until he was practically licking her face. Tilly laughed and stroked his forehead.

"That's more like it," she smiled. "So you like my bracelet, eh? Well, maybe I'll make one out of your hairs. You have such a beautiful tail. Jack Fisher is going to make you a champion one day, you'll see."

Red Admiral lifted his head and stood tall and proud, in the narrow shaft of sunlight. Then he started to nuzzle the horsehair bracelet again, almost chewing it off her wrist.

"Let me see your leg," Tilly whispered.

She leaned down beside his injured foreleg which was bandaged. She took the bandage off and instinctively she ran her hand down the back of his tendon. Gradually, with her fingers, she began to massage the area from the knee down to

the fetlock. As she did, Red Admiral
lowered his head and stood still.

Suddenly Tilly had that strange feeling
again, the same one she'd had with Magic
Spirit, as if everything else had disappeared
and only she and Red Admiral existed.
They were lost in the moment and only
aware of each other. So much so, that neither
of them noticed when Duncan walked in
and stood for a second, watching them.

Eventually Tilly re-bandaged the leg
and stood up. She patted Red Admiral on
the shoulder and then, careful not to get
behind him in case he decided to kick, she
ran her fingers through his tail. She
gathered up the loose hairs and put them in
her pocket, so that later she could weave
them into a bracelet.

"You'll be fine, Red. I know you will,"
she said, patting him one more time before
leaving the stable. "I'll see you again
soon."

Five

When Tilly got home, she spent two hours on the internet, looking up riding tips, so that she would know exactly what to do during her lesson next day. Her dad agreed to take her to the farm for two o'clock, as long she helped make supper. Tilly's mum had gone out with friends and wouldn't be back till late, but she had left instructions for cooking spaghetti bolognaise, which was always a popular choice in the Redbrow household.

Tilly was sitting at the computer, with Scruff, the family's long-haired Jack Russell, lying at her feet, chewing on his favourite squeaky toy, when her dad called up to her.

"Tiger Lil'! It's time to make dinner. You promised you'd help!"

But Tilly had just found a brilliant pony-lovers' chat room, where she could

post questions and get advice from other riders. She wasn't ready to finish.

"Five more minutes, Dad – please!"

She could hear her dad muttering something in the kitchen, followed by the sound of pots and pans being clanked about. He wasn't the best of cooks, which is probably why he'd asked for her help.

Fifteen minutes later, Tilly was still at the computer. She had lost track of time, typing responses to a chat room member called 'MyPonyRocks'. It was nice to be able to answer questions as well as ask them. She knew exactly what to say when MyPonyRocks typed:

Can u help?? I adore my twelve-year-old chestnut, but for some reason she gets ultra-nervous around other horses at her stables.

She's especially scared of the big ones. How can I make her more confident around other horses?

Tilly thought of how Duncan had helped Magic Spirit to gain more confidence around the other ponies and horses, by introducing him to a friendly miniature pony called Thumbalina. She quickly typed a reply:

Try introducing her to another friendly pony that is smaller than her, maybe a miniature or Shetland, to help build her confidence. We did this with my favourite horse, Magic Spirit. He was scared of other horses too. Now, he's much happier and really likes his new friend. Good luck.
Tilly. x

By the time Tilly got to the kitchen, the spaghetti bolognaise was ready, but there was mess everywhere. Mr Redbrow wasn't impressed.

"You took so long, Tiger Lil', I had to get Adam to help me."

Tilly glanced at Adam, who was standing at the sink, licking tomato sauce from his fingers. It was all over his face, and the worktop, and the floor, and the oven.

"You didn't help with the cooking," he grinned. "So you've got to tidy up!"

That night, Tilly dreamed she was
watching Red Admiral win his first race and
everyone was standing at the winning post
cheering him on. The jockey looked up
and waved at Tilly, as they crossed the
finishing line one length in front of the
second horse. Oddly, the jockey appeared
to be Tilly's best friend, Becky, who had
no interest in horses and often told Tilly
she was pony crazy.

It was morning before she knew it. Tilly woke up and yawned. She washed her face and went downstairs to the kitchen.

"Morning, Tilly. Did you sleep well? It was so stuffy in the night, I kept waking up . . . Why is there tomato sauce all over the fridge door?" said her mum, with a puzzled expression.

Tilly winced and said nothing.

"Looks like there's going to be a thunderstorm today – that should clear the air. Although I hope the rain doesn't spoil your shopping trip with Becky."

At first, Tilly didn't take in what her mum had said. She poured some orange juice into a glass and started thinking about whether the thunderstorm would affect her riding lesson with Angela. She hoped not.

"Dad's taking me to Silver Shoe at two o'clock today," she beamed. "Angela's going to give me my first riding lesson, to say thank you for all my hard work at the stables."

Mrs Redbrow put the coffee pot down on the table.

"Oh dear, Tilly. You must have forgotten . . ."

"Forgotten what?"

"Your shopping trip – to North Cosford – with Becky. You girls planned it weeks ago. You were so excited when I agreed to let you go to town on your own together."

With that, Tilly remembered. An awful sick feeling rose in her stomach. She knew how much Becky had been looking forward to their first proper girly shopping trip together – *without* adults. And she'd been looking forward to it too, but all the excitement of Silver Shoe Farm had distracted her.

Tilly's mum frowned.

"You can't let Becky down now. She's your best friend."

"But Angela's offered to give me a private lesson. I can't let *her* down either. This might be my only chance!"

"Oh, I'm sure they'll be other chances, Tilly. Don't you worry."

Tilly knew her mum was right. And she

knew it wasn't fair to cancel her plans with
Becky at such short notice, but she couldn't
help feeling disappointed. The lesson with
Angela had made her feel so overwhelmingly
happy – the thought of it not happening was
crushing. Then she thought of Mia and
Cally, going off to ride for the afternoon, or
the girls from Cavendish Hall, trotting
through the village on their perfect ponies.
She felt envious of them all. She couldn't
help it.

"It's not fair!" she said, standing up,
feeling suddenly tearful and angry. "This
is all I've ever wanted and now you're
making me miss it to go on a stupid
shopping trip with Becky!"

"Tilly!" said her mum, surprised by her daughter's outburst. "This isn't like you! I know how much you want to learn to ride, but it can't be the be all and end all."

"It *is*!" snapped Tilly, as she stormed out of the kitchen.

She found Scruff in the hallway, licking his paws, and before he had a chance to react, she pulled a long coat over her pyjamas, tugged on her trainers, grabbed his lead, clipped it to his collar, and marched out of the house.

Six

Just as Tilly's mum had predicted, the sky was thundery grey. It looked as if the clouds would burst any minute now, and soak everything. Tilly didn't care. She stomped up the road with a bewildered Scruff scampering to keep up with her. At first she didn't think about where she was going, but somehow she found herself heading for the road that led to Silver Shoe Farm.

"I'll walk *all* the way there," she hissed at Scruff, her teethed clenched.

Tilly knew she was only allowed to take Scruff for walks along the roads and pathways near Lower Norbury. Her mum and dad would be worried if they knew she was planning to go so far from the village. But she was too annoyed to think sensibly.

"It's not fair, Scruff! It's not fair!"

Scruff sniffed her ankles.

"Honestly, I didn't mean to say that the shopping trip with Becky was stupid – the words just came out of my mouth. I don't want to be horrible to her. She's my best friend . . . it's just . . ."

Tilly sighed.

"I really, *really* want to learn to ride. You understand don't you, Scruff?"

He looked up and wagged his tail.

The pair of them marched past the sign for Lower Norbury, and started along the narrow pavement of the busy road.

After ten minutes, a loud rumbling noise filled the air – the first clap of thunder. Scruff yapped nervously so Tilly picked him up. Seconds later, the

downpour started. Cold, fat raindrops
bounced off the leaves and the tarmac.

"Uh, oh!" cried Tilly, cuddling Scruff
tightly. "We're gonna get soaked!"

She glanced around, but the only
shelter was a bus stop up the road.

"I suppose it's better than nothing,"
she muttered, and ran through the rain
towards it. It didn't help that she was
still wearing her pyjamas!

By the time Tilly and Scruff reached the
bus stop, they were drenched. Several cars
zoomed past them, splashing up puddles of

water. They sat on a wooden bench and waited for the rain to stop. The thought of walking home, wet and cold, wasn't pleasant.

Tilly reached for her phone, thinking that her dad might be able to pick her up, but then she remembered that her phone was still in her jeans' pocket – and she was still in her pyjamas.

"What are we going to do *now*?" she shrugged, feeling silly and pathetic. Scruff put his head on her lap and whimpered.

The sight of the driving rain made Tilly wonder whether the Silver Shoe horses were outside getting wet, or whether they were all cosy in their stables. She knew that Magic Spirit wouldn't like the loud thunderclaps and hoped he wasn't too frightened. And what about poor Becky? Tilly pictured her, sitting at home, staring out of the window and worrying that the rain would spoil the shopping trip she'd been looking forward to for so long. She felt guilty.

Just then, a four-wheel drive pulled into the bus stop. The passenger window came

down. Tilly looked in and saw it was
Angela.

"Goodness me, Tilly!" she said. "What
are you doing out here in the rain? You're
shivering! Hop in. I'll give you a lift."

Relieved, Tilly climbed in. She was
almost too cold to speak. Angela reached
for a spare jacket on the back seat and
wrapped it around her shoulders.

"Who's this?" she said.

"He's called Scruff," Tilly whispered.
"He's our dog."

"He's sweet," said Angela. "Do your
parents know you've come all this way in
the rain? You're nearly at Silver Shoe – your
riding lesson isn't until two o'clock."

With that, Tilly started to cry. She was
so cold and confused she couldn't stop
herself, but Angela was very kind.

"Oh dear, what's happened?"

"I just wanted my first riding lesson,"
sobbed Tilly. "I forgot I was supposed to be
meeting Becky, and now I feel really bad . . .
and I want to do both . . . but there isn't

51

enough time . . . and no one knows that I came all this way . . . and I haven't got my phone with me . . . and now I'm so cold . . ."

Angela gave her a tissue and rubbed Tilly's shoulder until she was calm again.

"Okay, Tilly. How about this for a good plan? I'll ring your mum and dad and explain where you are, and we'll fix up another day for you to have a riding lesson. It doesn't have to be today – not if you've got other plans."

"But I thought this was my only chance . . . because you had a cancellation . . ."

"Of course not. I want to help you to learn to ride, Tilly. I think you've got a special talent with the horses. Let me talk to your mum and dad about it."

On the way back to the Redbrows' house, Tilly and Angela talked about lots of things, but particularly about riding and friendship and how important it was to have both.

"When I was younger," explained Angela, "I was always going off with my mates and forgetting to do my jobs around the stables. My dad and I argued constantly about it."

Tilly listened.

"Ever since I was a small kid I'd been working with the horses – every morning, every evening and every weekend. It was the family business. But when I was a

teenager, I rebelled. I realised how much I loved the horses in the end, though. My advice to you, Tilly, is to find a balance. You need horses in your life, but you also need your family and friends."

Tilly knew that Angela was talking lots of sense. She sat back and watched the windscreen wipers swish from side to side, and felt warm and happy again.

Seven

Tilly's parents were so relieved to see Tilly safe, they weren't cross with her for walking away from the village. As Angela's four-wheel drive pulled up, they waved from the front door.

"She looks like a drowned rat!" said Adam.

"You silly sausage!" said Tilly's mum, hugging her and kissing the top of her head. It was good to be home.

Mr Redbrow stood in the hallway

talking with Angela. Tilly wanted to hear what they were saying, but her mum was fussing so much, she rushed her straight upstairs for a hot bath.

By the time she came down again, Angela had gone.

"Don't worry," said her dad. "Angela has arranged another lesson for you, next Thursday after school. Although I suppose you'll want more than one, once you get the taste for it."

Tilly nodded, wide-eyed.

"How many lessons will she need?" asked Mrs Redbrow, as she ran a comb through Tilly's wet hair.

"Well, it depends how quickly she learns," explained her dad. "Angela said there are different kinds: group lessons, private tuition. We'll start with one and see how it goes."

Tilly had her fingers crossed again. The more lessons she had, the quicker she would improve, and the closer she'd get to the chance of one day owning her own horse.

After lunch, Tilly received a text from
Becky saying:

HEY T! CAN'T WAIT TO GO SHOPPING. WHAT ARE
YOU WEARING? X

She knew she'd done the right thing.
She quickly sent one back
saying:

SKINNY JEANS AND MY GREEN TOP.
CAN'T WAIT EITHER! SEE YOU SOON. X

Fortunately the rain had
stopped and the sky was blue
again. Tilly and her mum
drove to Becky's house,
picked her up, and then took
the short route into North
Cosford.

"Have a great time, girls,"
she said, as Tilly and Becky
got out of the car. "I'll meet
you back here at four-thirty."

58

Becky was so excited she tripped over the pavement, which made the pair of them burst into fits of giggles. Tilly's mum smiled and shook her head, then drove away.

"Freedom!" cried Becky, throwing her arms up in the air.

"Hurrah!" grinned Tilly. "Where first?"

"Let's go to Topshop, then Claire's Accessories, and then Debenhams. We can go to the beauty counters and try perfumes on!"

"Good plan – let's get bubble-gum slushies from the newsagent on the way."

"And strawberry laces."

"And maybe after Debenhams we can go to the riding shop on Green Street."

"If we must," groaned Becky. "But only if we can go to HMV after that – I want to look at CDs."

"Agreed."

Together, the girls tumbled into the newsagents and bought their sweets and slushies. Then they headed straight for the undercover shopping precinct.

In Topshop, Becky picked out armfuls of clothes to try on. Most of them were far too big for her, in adult sizes eight, ten and twelve, but she insisted she was hunting for a sophisticated look. She trailed up and down the aisles, with Tilly following.

"If I get through the auditions for *The X Factor*, I'll need to look super-stylish," Becky explained, as she stroked her hand across a gold sequined vest. "Oh, look! I saw this top in Mizz magazine – it's lush!

The girls stumbled into the changing rooms, and started matching things together, creating outfits for Becky to try on. Shiny blue trousers with a white shirt and a chunky belt. Baggy jeans with a cropped sailor jacket and stripy vest. A leopard print ball gown, with a giant bow, and neon green leggings.

"That's the one!" laughed Tilly. "That's the outfit that will get you noticed on *The X Factor*!"

"But I want them to notice my voice more than my outfit," said Becky, examining herself in the mirror. Too late, because

Tilly was distracted – she'd lost interest in the fancy party clothes and was daydreaming about wearing a smart dressage outfit: a top hat and a tail coat.

After visiting Claire's Accessories, where Tilly bought two sets of hair toggles for her plaits – one with lucky horseshoes and another with silver bows – they went to Pony Pride, the riding shop on Green Street.

The moment Tilly stepped inside, her eyes bulged. This was *her* kind of clothes shopping. The racks were full of the latest gear and accessories: denim-look jodhpurs, trendy gilets in pastel colours, quilted jackets and waterproofs, and polo shirts in every colour imaginable.

When she got to the boot section, Tilly was overwhelmed by the choice. There were jodhpur boots, long boots, waterproof

wellington boots, and even a range of
cowboy boots. Her eyes were drawn to a
pair of polished Toggi black zip-up jodhpur
boots. She took one of them off the shelf
and studied it. It smelled of new leather
and felt sturdy and comfortable.

The assistant came over and asked if Tilly needed help.

"That's a great boot," she explained. "Everyone's going for zips these days because it makes them so much easier to get on and off."

"How much are they?" asked Tilly.

"Very reasonable," the shop assistant replied, and told her the price.

Tilly gulped.

"Let's go and look at the grooming kits," she said, nudging Becky, who had found a seat and was looking bored.

To Tilly's relief, the grooming kits were much more affordable. Some of them came in lovely cases or bags, and had everything you would need: dandy brushes, curry combs, body brushes, hoof picks. Some of them came with a free supply of different sprays, to help release dirt and improve the shine on a horse's coat.

A kit of her own would be a great birthday present addition, along with the riding lessons, she thought.

Eventually, Becky started to huff and puff.

"Can we go?" she said. "There's only so much pony stuff I can handle, you know. I'm ready to go now."

"Come on then," said Tilly. "I'm ready too."

But really she could have stayed in that shop for hours.

Eight

On Thursday, Tilly got a lift to Silver Shoe with Mia's mum. They met at the school gates at four o'clock as usual. In the car they all talked excitedly about Tilly's lesson while they got changed into their stable clothes. Tilly pulled on her pink polo shirt and a pair of cream jodhpurs that Cally had given her.

"I bet you're a natural!" said Cally.

"Definitely," said Mia. "You'll be riding with us in no time."

I hope so, thought Tilly.

When they got to the stables, Tilly went over to the sand school where Angela was waiting with Bunny, the dapple grey pony that Mia and Cally had been riding last week.

"Hi, Tilly. This is Bunny Hop. I think she'll be perfect for your first lesson. She's only 13hh and very experienced. Her owner, Zoe, is in America, so I'm sure Bunny will appreciate the attention. Come and say hello."

Tilly climbed over the fence of the sand school. Her feelings were a mixture of excitement and nerves. She'd never been on a horse before and didn't want to make any mistakes, but at the same time, she was thrilled to be finally getting the chance.

Fortunately, Bunny looked reassuringly small and gentle. Angela checked Tilly's clothing and boots.

"You look great, so all you need is this," said Angela, handing Tilly a crash helmet with a black silk on it. "Try it on. If it doesn't fit I've got others."

Tilly fitted the hat to her head. It was just right. Angela adjusted the chin strap for her and tucked her plaits behind her shoulders.

"There. You look a proper young rider."

Tilly grinned from ear to ear. She wished her mum and dad could see her now.

"The first thing we need to do is learn how to mount. Once you're up and comfortable, we'll go for a little walk

around the school to give you a chance to get a feel for it. Does that sound okay?"

"Brilliant!" said Tilly.

Angela showed Tilly how to hold the reins and mane with one hand and the saddle with the other. Then she demonstrated how to place the ball of her foot into the stirrup and spring up and over with the other leg.

Angela made it look easy, but the first couple of times Tilly tried, she couldn't get enough lift. She stumbled back to the ground, frustrated with herself.

"Don't worry," said Angela. "That happens to everyone – you'll get used to it. Bunny won't mind how many times it takes. Try again. Really use your leg to lift yourself."

This time, following Angela's advice, Tilly managed to swing herself up and into the saddle in one smooth motion. It felt great. For a moment, she was so pleased with herself that she forgot to notice that for the first time ever, she, Tilly Redbrow, was actually sitting on a pony.

As Angela led Bunny around the school, Tilly concentrated on what her hands and feet and body were doing. She wanted to get everything right, but the effort was making her tense.

"Relax a bit," said Angela. "Get a feel for Bunny's movement beneath you. Good riding is all about balance and straightness. But if you try too hard you'll lose your natural sense of it. Bring your heels down in the stirrups and just think about sitting tall – as if a piece of string is attached to the top of your head, pulling you tall."

Tilly pushed her heels down and elongated her back. Immediately she felt more balanced and in control.

"That's it," encouraged Angela. "The majority of a horse's problems can usually be traced to a rider's poor position, so always focus on sitting straight and in balance. You'll get used to it with experience."

71

They walked several more circuits of
the sand school. Tilly had to keep
concentrating on the things that Angela had

taught her because they didn't come automatically, but it felt good nonetheless. They reached the fence and then Angela unclipped the lead rope.

"I think you're ready to try a circuit by yourself."

Tilly smiled and nodded, but inside she was a little bit nervous.

"Just a nice gentle walk," reassured Angela. "Try not to hold the reins too tightly, but don't let them get too long either – one of the most common problems is riders with too long a rein. Try with your leg to nudge her forward into a light rein contact."

She showed Tilly how to gather up a loop of rein close to Bunny's mane, but Tilly found it difficult to relax. Her forearms were rigid.

"What if she runs away from me?" she said anxiously.

"You'll be okay. Bunny knows what she's doing. She's very protective of her young riders. Think of your arm and the rein as a piece of elastic that runs straight through your hand to your elbow – your arm is like an extension of the rein. Bunny can feel the subtlest of movements along this piece of elastic, so the signals don't need to be over-exaggerated."

Tilly adjusted her grip and relaxed her arms. At the same time, she made an effort to sit up straight. It all seemed like a lot to remember, making her arms do one thing and her legs and back do another!

"Okay? Ready?"

Tilly nodded.

"Off you go."

Bunny walked on and Tilly could feel herself really riding. It wasn't anything like as fast and as graceful as she had imagined

74

in all those daydreams about galloping across the prairie on Magic Spirit. It wasn't easy, and it must have looked a bit clumsy, but it still felt amazing.

Nine

When the lesson was finished, Angela led them back to the stables where Duncan showed Tilly how to take off Bunny's tack.

"Every horse should have correctly fitting bridles and saddles," he explained. "So many people don't fit bridles properly. A horse's mouth is very sensitive and there's nothing worse than a bit that's hanging too low or too high. If the bit is the right size and in the right position, with the noseband sitting just below the cheekbone, then it

makes it much easier for the horse to take an even contact from the rein."

He showed Tilly how to run up the stirrups and then undo the girth. Before he took the saddle off he showed her how to fit it so that the pommel didn't sit too low over the horse's wither.

"Good soft leather that. Let's take this stuff back to the tack room, and I'll show you how to clean and take care of everything."

As they walked across the yard, Duncan glanced sideways at Tilly.

"I saw you talking to Red Admiral by the way," he said quietly, as though it was a secret.

Tilly blushed.

"Whatever you said, or did, well, it seems to have helped. It's extraordinary how much better he seems – the heat and filling have totally disappeared from his leg. Jack Fisher thinks he'll make it to the Cosford race meeting. Doubts he'll win, but at least he'll get a run. So what's your secret, Tilly?"

Tilly shrugged, because truthfully she didn't know. She felt fabulous though. She'd had her first riding lesson and Red Admiral had made great progress. Could things get any better?

The tack room was warm and smelled of old leather. Tilly loved it. She stared in wonder at the rows of bridles and reins hung neatly

on the wooden-panelled walls in three rows, and the different kinds of saddle racks on another wall: eventing saddles, unusual jumping saddles, dressage saddles. There was a saddle horse in the centre of the room and a hook where the bridles were cleaned before being hung up in their correct places. Duncan fetched a bucket of hot water and a sponge, and then the pair of them were ready to clean Bunny's tack.

"First of all, you need to remove any grease and dirt with a hot damp cloth – dirty tack can cause skin infections for the horse. Careful cleaning gives you a good chance to check the stitching and see that nothing is damaged or worn out."

Tilly wiped the equipment with a cloth and washed the bit and stirrup irons.

"Now use some saddle soap, which keeps everything supple – here."

He passed Tilly a damp sponge, which she rubbed across both sides of the saddle, and then he showed her how to apply a leather dressing on the underside.

"You only need to use leather dressing once a month. And obviously with synthetic tack, it isn't necessary at all."

"Do you think Magic Spirit will get his own tack?" she asked.

"Sure," said Duncan. "I'll have to start breaking him in soon. Although he's had some experience of being handled, he's got a long way to go before he's rideable. I think he'll be a tricky character to work with, but we'll see what we can do."

"Can I watch when you break him in?" asked Tilly eagerly.

"Watch? You'll be helping me, Tilly. Magic Spirit trusts you more than anyone. With your input I'm sure we'll eventually get a good response from him."

Suddenly the door of the tack room swung open. It was Cally and Mia returning from their ride, looking sweaty but pleased.

"Hey, Tilly! How was your lesson?"

"It was brilliant," said Tilly, buzzing. "Bunny's a sweet little pony, isn't she?"

"She's lovely," Tilly replied, pleased

that she could talk from experience now.

"So when's your next lesson? You've got to hurry up and get good, so that you can come out with us!" said Mia.

"No one needs to hurry up anything," interrupted Duncan firmly. "Tilly will learn to ride in her own time. There's no need to rush."

"I know, I know," said Mia, playfully flicking his baseball cap. Cally kept quiet. She always did around Duncan. Tilly knew this was because she had a crush on him.

"But seriously, Tilly," added Mia. "When is your next lesson? We'll come and watch."

Tilly looked at the ceiling.

"Um, I don't know. It depends on whether my mum and dad agree to get me lessons for my birthday or not."

"Your birthday! You didn't tell us it was your birthday! When?"

"June the twenty-first."

"That's the day of the Cosford races," grinned Mia. "You'll have to join us – loads of people from Silver Shoe are going. We go every year – it's really fun and everyone gets dressed up. You're going to be racing, aren't you, Duncan?"

"That's right. You should definitely join us. I'm sure there'll be room in one of the cars for a little one," he said, smiling at Tilly.

Ten

When Tilly woke up on the twenty-first of June, she had a feeling that it would be a doubly good day. Not only because it was her birthday, but because she was going to the Cosford races to watch Red Admiral race.

Adam was the first to wish her a happy birthday, pouncing on her bed and singing:

"Happy birthday to you,
Squashed tomatoes and poo,
I saw a fat monkey,
And I thought it was you!"

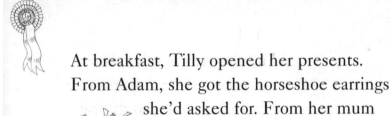

At breakfast, Tilly opened her presents.
From Adam, she got the horseshoe earrings
she'd asked for. From her mum
and dad, she got a pair of
smart denim-look jodhpurs,
like the ones she'd seen in
the shop. She tried them on
and they fitted perfectly.

"Thanks, Mum. Thanks, Dad," she
said, kissing them both, and
admiring her reflection in the
mirror.

"There's one more
thing," said her dad, pulling
an envelope out of his pocket.

Tilly held her breath. Could this be the
riding lessons she'd been hoping for?

She quickly tore open the
envelope. Inside was a Pony
Club leaflet.

"We've bought you special
membership to the Cosford
branch," said her mum, smiling.
"Angela recommended it. She

said all the girls at Silver Shoe are members. They organise rallies and events, and during the school holidays they run special camps. You can borrow a pony from the stables. Won't that be fun?"

"That's ace. Thanks, Mum."

But although Tilly was thrilled with her Pony Club membership, she couldn't help worrying that the thing she wanted most of all had been forgotten about – riding lessons.

She decided not to say anything, in case it made her mum and dad feel bad. They'd got her so many lovely things, it seemed greedy to ask for more. Instead, she studied the Pony Club leaflet and tried to put it out of her mind.

Tilly got a lift to the Cosford race course
with Mia's mum and dad, who were both
dressed glamorously and arguing about
which horses they were going to place bets
on. Tilly, Mia and Cally sat in the back
seat, discussing Duncan's tactics. He was
riding Red Admiral in the Cosford
Champion Hurdle.

When they arrived, the place was bustling with activity. Several huge marquees lined the track and there were hoards of smartly-dressed people chatting and laughing in groups and waving their race cards about.

Tilly and the girls made their way through the crowds and leaned up against the barrier so that they could get a good look at the race.

"It looks like a green velvet carpet!" gasped Cally. There wasn't a blade of grass out of place.

"Imagine flying those hurdles and galloping up to the finishing line – it would be like riding Pegasus!"

"Wow!" they all said together.

"Hello, girls," said a voice behind them. It was Angela. She was wearing a suit and had her hair pinned back with a flower clip. She looked very pretty.

"Hi, Angela."

"Where's Red Admiral?" said Cally excitedly. "Can we see him?"

"Not right now, I'm afraid. He's in the saddling enclosure. He'll be walked around the parade paddock in twenty minutes. They lead the horses around the paddock before a race so that everyone can view the runners and choose which ones they might place their money on."

"Is Duncan nervous?" asked Mia.

"No, well, at least, if he is, he doesn't show it."

"Do you think he and Red Admiral will win?" asked Tilly.

"Hmm, that's a tricky one. Red Admiral loves firm ground, so the dry weather will suit him. But he hasn't raced for a long time, so that will probably slow him down. We didn't think he'd make it for this race, but weirdly his leg has come right in the nick of time."

Tilly didn't say anything. She just twisted the horsehair bracelet she'd made from Red Admiral's tail and tried to send positive thoughts to him and Duncan.

"Come and join the Silver Shoe crowd

in the enclosure, girls. We've got a great view of the finish."

Tilly insisted she wanted to wish Red Admiral luck before the race, so she went to see him being led round the paddock by Jack. His coat was gleaming and he looked majestic. To top it all, he wore the number seven on his saddle cloth – Tilly's lucky number.

Suddenly a bell rang to signal to the jockeys that it was time to mount their horses. There were nerves all round. Jack hoped that Red was fit, plus this was the first race that Duncan was to ride for Silver Shoe Farm – something he had only ever dreamed about. The Brigdales, Red Admiral's owners, had kept their promise and allowed Red to stay at Silver Shoe Farm as a thank you for all the hard work that had gone into his rehabilitation.

The Brigdales were in the middle of the paddock with Duncan, who was wearing their familiar colours of green with a yellow cross and a white silk cap over his crash helmet. As the jockeys mounted Tilly could see the owners wishing them luck and the trainers giving them last words of advice.

Jack sensibly told Duncan to ride Red Admiral according to how he felt – not to push him hard, but if it felt good at the halfway point, to let him run. They circled the paddock one last time before going out onto the course.

Just as Tilly was regretting she hadn't wished Duncan or Red good luck, they stopped directly in front of her. Red affectionately nudged her arm and

Tilly whispered to him, "Go like the wind, but above all, keep safe!" Then she looked up and wished Duncan luck.

By the time Tilly had caught up with everyone in the members' enclosure, the horses had cantered down to the start. There were lots of familiar faces from Silver Shoe Farm, all whispering and smiling and giving thumbs-up gestures. Jack Fisher was standing quietly at the side, his arms folded, a little apart from everyone else. Tilly tugged her bracelet and sent positive thoughts to him too.

The commentator announced that the horses were under starter's orders. A hush spread across the crowd and Tilly could feel the atmosphere bristle.

"Oh, crumbs!" whispered Mia. "It's *too* exciting."

She grabbed Tilly's hand and squeezed it. Cally, standing next to her, was jiggling up and down.

"Don't get your hopes up," said Mia's dad, who had stepped in behind them. "I've heard the Silver Shoe Farm horse is a non-starter."

"Shhh!" hissed Mia. "What do you

know about it anyway, Dad?"

"I know I've got thirty quid riding on it," he growled.

"Lucky Francis takes up the running!" said the commentator, as the horses approached the first flight of hurdles. They cleared it with ease and thundered onto the second flight. There were seventeen horses in the race and at this early stage Red Admiral lay mid-field travelling with ease.

Tilly couldn't believe how stylish Duncan looked, like a professional who had been racing for years. As the horses approached halfway, the crowd grew louder and louder, urging the horses they had bet on to run faster.

It upset Tilly to see a nasty fall at the sixth flight of hurdles, but thankfully both horse and rider were soon on their feet. She kept nervously twiddling her Red

Admiral bracelet, willing every stride to become longer and longer.

With just two hurdles to go, she hoped he was in with a chance, but after hearing everyone's doubts, she knew it was unlikely they would win. She glanced over at Jack Fisher, who was chewing his nails, eyes glued to the course.

"Go on, Red Admiral! Go on, Duncan!" yelled Cally and Mia.

"Yes!" yelled Mia's dad, punching the air with his fist as Red Admiral started to come up through the field of runners.

It wasn't over yet. There was still one more flight of hurdles on the home straight. Red Admiral was neck and neck with a steely grey horse called Morning Frost. The commentator was shouting enthusiastically. The crowd was going wild as they cleared the last alongside each other.

He can't be beaten at this stage in the race, thought Tilly, closing her eyes.

"Come on, Red – faster, faster, you can

do it!" she bellowed at the top of her voice.

Instantly, as if Red had heard her, he surged forward lowering his head and neck. He galloped past Morning Frost and crossed the finishing line with a horse's length between them.

The sound of cheering followed and Tilly immediately opened her eyes. She could just about make out Duncan, smiling from ear to ear as he patted Red Admiral on the shoulder. It was good news!

The commentator announced the first three places. To hear the words: 'First: Red Admiral' was music to the ears of everyone at Silver Shoe Farm.

"Red Admiral is the winner of the seventeenth annual Cosford Champion Hurdle! What a horse!"

The Silver Shoe gang roared with delight. Mia's dad threw his programme into the air and started dancing around, singing

'Who wants to be a millionaire!' People everywhere were laughing and hugging each other.

In the corner, Tilly spotted Jack Fisher, standing alone and smiling to himself. She slipped through the happy crowd and approached him.

"Well done, Mr Fisher! You did it!" she said quietly.

"And well done to you, Tilly! You did it too!" he nodded, with a knowing glint in his eye.

Eleven

"I think this has been the best birthday ever," said Tilly, as they arrived back at Silver Shoe Farm, where she was expecting to be picked up by her mum and dad. She noticed their car was parked in the lane, but they were nowhere to be seen.

"It's not over yet," said Mia.

"What do you mean?" said Tilly.

"Um, do you think you could help us muck out Rosie's stall quickly? We didn't get a chance to do it this morning."

"Oh, er, yeah. I guess," said Tilly obligingly, although she wasn't exactly keen on the idea of shovelling manure after such a thrilling day.

"Thanks," said Cally and Mia together, eyes sparkling.

Tilly trudged over to the stables and picked up a fork and shovel. She was confused as to why Cally and Mia weren't coming to help her. And she couldn't help wondering where her mum and dad had disappeared to? Suddenly it seemed as though everyone was behaving oddly. Even Angela was rushing about and didn't stop to say hello.

She went into the tack room to fetch some water and a broom, and

104

when she came out the yard was empty.
She walked over to the stables, opened the
door and went inside.

"SURPRISE!" came a chorus of voices.
"Happy birthday, Tilly!"

The stable was lined with banners and
ribbons. Everyone, including Tilly's mum
and dad, and her best friend Becky,

were waving at her. They were wearing party hats, and some of the horses who didn't mind were wearing them too. Tilly laughed and put the fork down.

"Here, have some birthday cake," said Angela. "I made it myself – it was my mum's old recipe."

"We've even got a special cake for the horses," said Cally, pointing to an enormous slab of seeds and honey.

They all sat down on bales of hay and ate cake and drank homemade lemonade. The combination was delicious.

"So this is where you spend all your time," said Becky, smiling. "It's quite cool actually. Here, I got you this."

Becky handed Tilly a present. Tilly unwrapped it and inside was one of the grooming kits she'd admired in the riding shop.

"Thanks, Becky!"

"I thought you'd like it – after you drooled all over it in that shop!"

Tilly giggled.

Twenty minutes later, the sound of an engine purred in the yard.

"Hey! They're back!" said Mia.

Everyone got up and went outside, to where Duncan was leading Red Admiral out of the horse box. Angela rushed over and kissed Duncan on the cheek. Tilly, Mia and Cally nudged each other.

"I hear you were fantastic," said Mr Redbrow, smiling at Duncan as he patted Red Admiral on the shoulder.

"Oh, thanks, but it wasn't just down to me. I had a bit of help," he said, nodding at Tilly. "Happy birthday. Did you enjoy watching your first race?"

"It was brilliant!" said Tilly. "Here, I made you this."

She handed Duncan the horsehair bracelet she had made from Red Admiral's tail.

"Oh, thanks, Tilly. How thoughtful. So, what about you? Did you get those riding lessons you wanted?"

"Oh, um, not exactly," said Tilly,

awkwardly. "But that's okay," she shrugged, trying to hide her disappointment.

"Hang on a minute," said her dad suddenly. "I nearly forgot. Your other present, Tiger Lil'. . ."

"What other present?" asked Tilly.

"Ah ha," said Angela stepping forward. "Your parents and I have been doing some talking. We know how much you want riding lessons and, well, we've agreed that you can have as many as you need."

"But that will be so expensive for you," said Tilly, looking at her parents.

"It's okay," said her mum. "We'll pay for weekly lessons, and then Angela said she'd try to give you a bit of extra tuition for free. She thinks you've got such an extraordinary gift with the horses that it shouldn't be wasted."

"*Really?*" gasped Tilly.

"You'll have to work hard," said Angela cautiously. "But I know you won't mind that."

"Of course I won't," said Tilly, throwing

her arms around her mum and dad, and then Angela.

Mia and Cally clapped their hands together. They were almost as pleased as Tilly was.

"I was wrong when I said I think this has been the best birthday ever," said Tilly, stroking Red Admiral's nose.

"Actually, I know it's the best birthday ever!"

And with that, everyone cheered.

Pippa's Top Tips

Make sure the head collar is comfortable for your pony.
When fitting it, always be careful to avoid their eyes,
ears and nose, and don't make it too tight. Head collars
are always fitted more loosely than bridles.

Horses can be unpredictable creatures, so you should
always take care around them. For example, never loop
the lead rope around your hand. If your pony pulls away
suddenly, you risk injuring your hand.

Good riding is all about balance and straightness, and
the majority of a horse's problems can usually be traced
to a rider's poor position.

Always sit tall, as if a piece of string is attached to
the top of your head, pulling you up.

Establish a light rein contact. Think of your arm and the
rein as a piece of elastic that runs through your hand to
your elbow. Your pony can feel the slightest of
movements along the rein, so your signals don't need to
be over-exaggerated.

A pony's mouth is very sensitive and there's nothing worse than an ill-fitting bit. The bit should be just the right size and position, with the noseband sitting just below the cheek bone.

Hosing your pony's leg can help reduce a swelling if he's taken a knock, but always get a vet to check out any injuries.

Dirty tack can cause skin infections for a horse, so always clean your tack after riding. First, remove any grease and dirt with a hot, damp cloth, then use some saddle soap to keep everything supple.

Careful cleaning also gives you a good chance to check the stitching and see that nothing is damaged or worn out. You should apply a leather dressing to the underside of the tack once a month – but, of course, this won't be necessary for synthetic tack.

Joining your local Pony Club is a great way to learn all the skills you need to care for your horse. They organise rallies and events, and some even run special camps during the school holidays.

For more about Tilly and Silver Shoe Farm – including pony tips, quizzes and everything you ever wanted to know about horses – visit www.tillysponytails.co.uk